# Abuela's LIBRARY

Written by **Lissette Norman**     Illustrated by **Jayri Gómez**

**HARPER**

*An Imprint of HarperCollinsPublishers*

Every Saturday, Abuela and I go to the library to find the perfect book. Afterward, we sit under our favorite oak tree in front of our building.

Nobody loves books more than Abuela.
She was a school librarian once.
She says books hold this world together and you
can never have too many.

In our shady spot, Abuela and I read the whole afternoon away.
Then a worker gets out of a truck with the words *Uptown Gas &*
*Electric* painted on the door.

"This oak is leaning close to our power line,"
he says. "If it falls, it'll knock out the electricity
in this neighborhood."

"But this is one of the strongest trees
on our street," I say.

"It's hard to tell that it's sick," he explains. "But if you look way up top, you can see the dead branches."
"What will happen to it?" Abuela asks.
"We'll have to cut it down."

Men come in big trucks a week later.
Piece by piece, they cut my and Abuela's
special tree down to a stump.

From my bedroom window, I stare down at the
stump that once was more. I wonder if it misses
the birdsongs and squirrels.
And if, maybe, it misses Abuela and me too.

I remember the barred owl that used to
nest inside the tree hole.
That's when I get an idea to turn that
stump into something magical.

"Abuela, what if we put a library *inside* the tree stump?"
I show her my drawing of a little library with a door as
blue as the sky.

"Alfonso, that's a fantastic idea!"
she says, just as excited as I am.

I show my drawing to my friends, hoping they'll help.

"That's crazy!" Johnny says.

"You can't put a library in there," says my neighbor Giselle.

But Papi nearly jumps off the sofa.
"Let me gather my tools and we'll start tomorrow!" he says.
"We'll hang lights on it for all to see," Mami says.

We start building the library on Saturday.

Step #1:
Papi carves a hole out of
the middle of the huge stump.

Step #2:
Abuelo cuts wood in
different sizes for the door, the
slanted roof, and the shelves.

Step #3:
Mami and I nail wood together to make the door. Then we add pieces of glass in the center so you can see inside the library.

Step #4:
Abuela and Papi lay wooden shingles in neat rows on the roof.

We work until the sun sinks behind our tall building.

The next day, Giselle and her father stop
by to see what we're doing.
"Wow, you really *can* put a library inside
a stump!" Giselle says. "Can we help?"

Step #5:
Giselle and I paint the library
door sky-blue and white.

Step #6:
Abuelo nails the shelves inside the stump hole.

Step #7:
Giselle's dad and Papi hang the door.

Step #8:
Mami and Abuela decorate the library with fairy lights and lanterns.

Step #9:
I fill the shelves with all the books I chose.

When we're done, we stand back and look at our little neighborhood library, so proud.

Kids visit our little library each day.
They give and take books.
They ask me questions about what to read and I help them find something they might like.

This is how my love for matching people with the perfect book begins. It's how I know I will be a librarian one day too.

To my literary agent, Johanna Castillo,
and her son, Alfonso, with love and deep gratitude.

And to all librarians, who guide us to other worlds, to the
unlooked for, to what we love, and to what loves us in return.
—L.N.


To my siblings, Lia, Enya, and Jariel.
Although I don't say it much, I love you.
—J.G.

WARNING: Children should never use
building tools without careful adult supervision.

Abuela's Library

Text copyright © 2024 by Lissette Norman

Illustrations copyright © 2024 by Jayri Gómez

All rights reserved. Manufactured in Italy.

No part of this book may be used or reproduced in any manner whatsoever without written permission except
in the case of brief quotations embodied in critical articles and reviews. For information address HarperCollins
Children's Books, a division of HarperCollins Publishers, 195 Broadway, New York, NY 10007.

www.harpercollinschildrens.com

Library of Congress Control Number: 2022952378

ISBN 978-0-06-306753-0

The artist used Procreate to create the digital illustrations for this book.

Typography by Rachel Zegar

24  25  26  27  28   RTLO   10  9  8  7  6  5  4  3  2  1

First Edition